A GIANT
THANK YOU TO:
JENNY, IZZY AND EMMA
FOR ALL YOUR
HARD WORK.

LIZ X

FOR HOLLY AND DAISY
WHO LOVE JELLY BEANS!

AND FOR DAD, HELEN
AND MUM

WITH ALL MY LOVE

X❀ X❀ X❀ X❀ X❀

tiger tales

5 River Road, Suite 128, Wilton, CT 06897

Published in the United States 2014

Originally published in Great Britain 2014

by Hodder Children's Books

a division of Hachette Children's Books

Text copyright © 2014 Rachael Mortimer

Illustrations copyright © 2014 Liz Pichon

ISBN-13: 978-1-58925-136-6

ISBN-10: 1-58925-136-9

Printed in China

WKT1013

10 9 8 7 6 5 4 3 2 1

For more insight and activities, visit us at www.tigertalesbooks.com

Jack and the
Jelly Bean Stalk

by Rachael Mortimer

Illustrated by Liz Pichon

tiger tales

Jack's mother shook the flour barrel and peered inside the cookie tin. She looked in dismay at the last few crumbs.

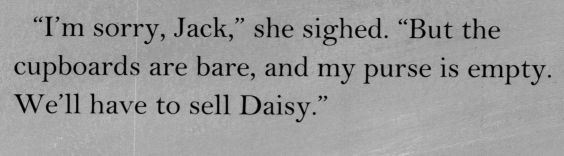

"I'm sorry, Jack," she sighed. "But the cupboards are bare, and my purse is empty. We'll have to sell Daisy."

"Don't worry, Mother," said Jack sadly. "I'll get a good price for her."

Daisy was the cutest cow you ever did see. So it wasn't surprising that even before they got to town, a farmer had offered Jack twenty gold coins for her.

"Twenty gold coins!"
His mother would be so pleased.

Jack was on his way home when all of a
sudden, he spotted a wonderful candy store.

Inside, there were...

JUICY JELLIES

FRUIT SOURS

GOOEY GUMS

HEAPS OF LOLLIPOPS

CHUNKY CHOCOLATE RAISINS

YUMMY PINEAPPLE CHUNKS

RAINBOW CHEWS

STRAWBERRY STRAWS

But Jack could not take his eyes off
an enormous bag of glittering jelly beans!

LA

"These are magic beans, in every flavor you could wish for!" smiled the shopkeeper. "And for twenty gold coins, you can have them all!"

Jelly Beans
WARNING
may contain
smelly sock beans

AMAZING
Jelly Beans

TREATS

Every flavor he could wish for!
Jack couldn't help himself.
He handed over his money.

Jack walked home in a dream.
But when he arrived home without
Daisy and without any money,
his mother was furious.

"You silly boy! What use are jelly beans?"

She threw the bag outside and sent Jack straight to bed without any supper.

In the middle of the night, Jack woke to a delicious smell

of blueberries, chocolate, strawberries, ice cream,

and caramel wafting in through his window.

A **giant** jelly bean stalk was growing in his garden!

It was a beautiful sight—shining in the moonlight, covered in brightly-colored beans in all the yummy flavors he had ever dreamed of!

Jack opened his window and began to climb, cramming jelly beans in his mouth as he went—apple, pear, mint, sherbet, chocolate chip, apple pie, cotton candy, popcorn….

Higher and higher he climbed, until feeling rather full,
he came to a huge golden gate and a large sign.

Jack was hesitating when
he heard a strange noise.
He peered inside the door....

"Honk! Honk!" sobbed a little white goose. "The Giant is so angry. I've tried my best to lay more golden eggs, but it's just no good! The pantry is empty, and there's nothing to eat in the castle except me and that stringy old harp!"

Suddenly, the ground shook!

"*Fee-fi-fo-foy,*
I smell a juicy boy!
Goose is good, but boy's so tasty.
Served with chips and
wrapped in pastry!"

"Stop!" stuttered Jack as the Giant scooped him up in his hand. "I'm very bony, and I haven't washed for weeks. Give me ten minutes and I'll bring you a banquet—a feast fit for a king!"

"Hmmm...," said the Giant, putting Jack back down again.

"My clock is ticking. Tick, tick, tick! Bring my feast and make it quick!"

Jack had never worked
so fast! In ten minutes,
he had picked hundreds
of jelly beans.

The giant had melon beans for his starter and French fry beans for his main course. It was all washed down with a fruity bean smoothie. The goose watched hungrily.

The Giant was just about to dive into his chocolate pudding beans when…

...the goose swallowed
them down whole.

Honk!

The Giant was furious!
He grabbed the goose
and shook her.

Honk!

Honk!

Honk!

But the beans would not come out!

He threw her down to grab his carving knife, and Jack grabbed the goose and raced for the jelly bean stalk....

"Stop!" yelled the Giant, thundering after them.

He grabbed the stalk and tried to climb down but he was much too heavy. The jelly bean stalk began to sway. It wibbled and wobbled…

...then came crashing
to the ground.

CRASH!

Jack looked around and grinned.

The garden was covered in jelly beans.

The goose never laid another golden egg. But she did lay delicious speckled ones, tutti-fruity ones, and tingy-tangy ones.

Jack and his mother had enough jelly beans to feed them for years! Although every so often, they would find one that tasted like…